SUZU AND THE BRIDE DOLL

by

Patricia Miles Martin

Illustrated by Kazue Mizumura

More than anything in all Japan, Suzu wanted to hold the bride doll that stood in the case in her Grandmother's house. Tomorrow was the day she had waited for all year — the Festival of Dolls. Grandmother had many other beautiful dolls, but Suzu loved the bride doll the most. After her Grandmother had stepped into her jinrickisha to go to the Street of Shops, Suzu heard a voice — it was the voice of the bride doll. She wanted to get out to find her bridegroom from whom she had been separated, and she knew he was in Mr. Yamamoto's shop. She climbed on the back of the bronze crane and flew away. She found her bridegroom but he had to be sold before he could leave the shop. What do you suppose happened before the Festival of Dolls that made it the most wonderful one of all for Suzu?

* *

Dewey Decimal Classification: F

About the Author:

PATRICIA MILES MARTIN comes from Kansas, she has lived in Colorado and Wyoming, and taught school in those states. She and her husband now live in California. One of her hobbies is Oriental culture, and this book grew out of her love of the Far East. Another of her books, *The Pointed Brush,* a story with a Chinese background, was a New York Herald Tribune Honor Book.

About the Illustrator:

KAZUE MIZUMURA was born near Tokyo, Japan, and educated at the Peeresses' School in that city. After World War II and during the Occupation, she taught Japanese Sumi painting to GI students from the Army Education Center. A scholarship from Pratt Institute brought her to the United States.

SUZU

AND THE BRIDE DOLL

by PATRICIA MILES MARTIN

illustrated by KAZUE MIZUMURA

1964 FIRST CADMUS EDITION
THIS SPECIAL EDITION IS PUBLISHED BY ARRANGEMENT WITH
THE PUBLISHERS OF THE REGULAR EDITION
RAND McNALLY & COMPANY
BY
E. M. HALE AND COMPANY
EAU CLAIRE, WISCONSIN

More than she wanted anything else in all of Japan, Suzu wanted to hold the doll that stood in the case in her grandmother's house.

Under the parakeet's bamboo cage, beside the bronze crane on the low table, was the case with the sliding panels that held the bride doll.

As long as Suzu could remember, the doll and the bronze crane were displayed each year to celebrate the Festival of the Dolls. But Suzu had never held the doll—the lovely bride doll whose face was the color of whitest chalk.

Tomorrow, the third day of the third month, was the day for which Suzu had long been waiting. Tomorrow was the day of the Festival of the Dolls.

The festival would be celebrated in almost every house in Japan. In each house, there would be shelves in the alcove, with festival dolls in their proper places on the shelves.

Suzu and Grandmother were busy getting ready for the festival. Their own shelves stood in their alcove. Grandmother had spread a long length of bright red silk that reached from the highest shelf down to the lowest.

Two small folding screens stood in the middle of the
top shelf, where the Emperor and Empress, two dolls of
great age and dignity, sat in royal splendor.

On the shelf beneath the royal dolls, three ladies from
the court sat waiting. And still below, five handsome,
dark-eyed musician dolls held flute and drums in their
hands.

Suzu looked at the lower shelves. These were the shelves she liked best. Here, the bride doll would stand between two toy trees, orange and cherry. She would stand among all the tiny and wonderful things a bride might need for her dowry—the little fan, the small charcoal stove, dainty chopsticks.

Suzu looked at each tiny piece—little cups and bowls, the small chest of drawers, the lovely little two-wheeled jinrickisha with its polished shafts.

Tomorrow, Suzu would prepare little green-colored
rice cakes. She would serve the dolls herself.

If only she might hold the bride doll.

Suzu looked at her grandmother. "Oba-chan,
Grandmother dear," she said. "Will you let me take the
bride doll from her case?"

Grandmother shook her head. "Perhaps she is the work of a great artist. I have never seen another like her. The doll may be . . ."

"But Oba-chan, I will be gentle and careful. Please."

"Do not interrupt." Grandmother's voice was kind. "Remember, politeness is a virtue. The doll may be as rare as a precious pearl. Remember, please."

"But why must she always stay in the case, except on festival days?" Suzu's heart was sad.

"She remains there so that no dust can touch the silk of her kimono, nor careless hand harm her." Grandmother smiled. "Do not be sad," she said. "You have your play dolls. See that they are ready for tomorrow. Then, go out into the garden and cut three branches of blossoms. Place them near the alcove, and let it seem that a small tree grows there."

"Yes, Oba-chan." Suzu's voice was low.

"When this is done," Grandmother said, "you will play the samisen. Remember to move your hands with grace when you pluck the strings."

"Yes, Oba-chan."

"Now I go to the Street of the Shops," Grandmother said. "Perhaps I shall bring back a small surprise for you." She slid open the door and stepped outside.

Suzu followed and helped Grandmother slip her feet out of soft house slippers and into the wooden sandals for street.

"I am going," Grandmother said.

Suzu watched while Grandmother stepped into a jinrickisha and raised her bright parasol. The wheels creaked as the runner started down the avenue. Suzu watched until they were out of sight.

She thought of the surprise Grandmother might bring. She wondered what it might be. What surprise could she bring that would be half so nice as being allowed to take the bride doll from her paper case? "That is what I want most of all," Suzu thought.

She gathered her play dolls together. There was black-eyed Maya. "Do not think I love the bride doll more," she whispered. "You are little and very dear to me."

There was laughing-eyed Tsuyako. "Do not think I love the bride doll more," she whispered. "You are gay and very precious."

There was Sachiko with her lovely hair. "Do not think I love the bride doll more," Suzu said. "You were my first doll."

She laid a floor cushion near the alcove.

"You, Maya and Tsuyako, you shall sit on the cushion and celebrate the festival, and Sachiko shall sit close beside." She placed the dolls on the cushion.

"There!" she said.

Outside, Suzu cut three branches. "My heart is joyous
again," she said. "When I am busy, I feel like laughing."

Inside the house, she sang a little tune as she arranged the flowers for the festival.

When each branch was in its proper place, Suzu settled herself on a cushion, her feet tucked neatly beneath her. Now she would play upon the samisen.

Suddenly, she heard a voice. The voice was small and it was high and clear. "Let me out, please!"

Suzu looked around the room, but there was nothing there, nothing at all. Only the parakeet swung on his perch, chattering in his gay little voice.

The high voice spoke again. "Are you never going to hear, Suzu? Must I remain locked here forever, because you will not listen?"

Suzu jumped to her feet and leaned on the low table,
her face close to the bride doll's case.

"Do you hear me?" the voice said.

"Oh yes, yes," Suzu said eagerly. "I hear you very well,
and I understand every word that you say."

"Then lift the panel of my case, please," the doll said.

"I don't think Grandmother would like it," Suzu said. "You see, you may be the work of a great artist. You are rare as a precious pearl."

"Suzu, Suzu! Can you imagine what it is like to live in a paper house, never to smell the iris in bloom, never to see the wisteria in the garden?" The doll's voice was pleading. "Please, Suzu!"

"What shall I do?" Suzu thought. "If I open the case, what will happen?"

"Please, Suzu!"

Trembling, Suzu lifted the panel.

The doll moved her arms gracefully and opened her folding fan. "I thought you were never going to hear," she said. She closed her fan with a little snap. "Have you never heard me calling before this? Never at all?"

Suzu shook her head. "I have only heard the parakeet talking in his cage."

The doll took two little shuffling steps and turned
to look over her shoulder. "Is the bow of my obi
properly tied?"

Suzu looked at the little sash. "It is properly tied," she
said. "You are the most beautiful bride doll I have
ever seen."

The doll bowed. "I am only Miyoko," she said, "a
bride doll who longs to find her bridegroom doll."

"Oh, then somewhere there is a bridegroom doll?"
Suzu asked.

"Of course!" Miyoko laughed, and her laughing was
like the tinkling of a bell. "All brides have bridegrooms."
Her face grew solemn. "Once, long ago, we stood side
by side in the house of a wealthy nobleman, and one
day the nobleman saw two pretty little girls playing in
the shade of the plum tree in his garden. To one small
girl he gave the bridegroom doll, and he gave me
to the other. That other was the grandmother who keeps
me in the case."

The bride doll stepped down from the platform. "Now that you have lifted the panel, I am free to go find Husband, who has been waiting for me so long. I have wished for this day."

"No, no!" Suzu thought of Grandmother. "You can't go away. If Grandmother returns and finds you gone, she will not be pleased. Not at all."

"Do not worry," Miyoko said. "I shall be gone a short time only. You will see. I wish to find Husband before the Festival of the Dolls. I know exactly where to find him. I shall bring him back with me."

"But how can you know where to go, when Japan is so big?" Suzu asked. "How can you know?"

"I was told by our parakeet, who heard it from a sparrow, who heard it from a house mouse. Husband is in Mr. Yamamoto's shop on the Street of the Shops. He sits high on a very dusty shelf between a big, black dragon and a small lute. Sometimes he plays the lute and sings of me. The house mouse heard the song. I shall go there."

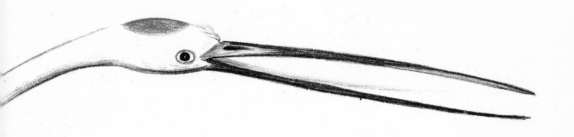

"But the Street of the Shops is so far." Suzu looked at the hem of the bride doll's kimono, folded close around her small ankles. "And your feet are so small." Suzu wished that Miyoko would climb back on the wooden platform in the case, and allow the panel to be slid into place again.

"No place is very far," Miyoko said, "when one travels with the bronze crane."

Suzu looked at the crane. He too, had suddenly come to life. He was flexing his wings and spreading them wide and balancing high on his feet.

Enchanted, Suzu watched while Miyoko settled herself on the crane's broad back.

With a loud whirring and beating of wings, they were off.

Suzu ran to the doorway. Already they were far beyond the little pine tree in the garden. So far away were they that she could barely see them against the blue of the sky.

She knelt on a floor cushion and tried to play the samisen, but one string sounded like the other and the music was not sweet.

She went outside and sat on a flat stone beside the pool and listened to the crowing of a small bantam rooster.

In the town, the bronze crane flew along the narrow
Street of the Shops.

When the bride doll saw a big blue sign with bold
white characters painted on it, she called out.

"Here is the shop! Mr. Yamamoto's. So it says on
the sign. Stop, please!"

The crane dipped in his flight and swooped into the
shop. The flutter of his wings set the wind chimes
tinkling and the shopkeeper's bell rang high and sweet.

Away up high near the ceiling, the crane lighted
on a dusty shelf where a bridegroom doll sat sprawled
against the wall, a price tag on his kimono.

The bride doll bowed low. "Husband," she said,
"do you remember Miyoko?"

Before he could answer, the shopkeeper came
running into the shop with great noisy steps, and the
bronze crane hid behind a great, black dragon. Miyoko
stood very still. She heard the shopkeeper talking to
himself.

"There is no one here," he said. "No one. Strange.
I thought I heard the shop bell ring and the wind
chimes tinkle."

Miyoko peeked at the bridegroom doll, but he did
not move. His smile was gentle.

The wind chimes tinkled again and Miyoko stood there without moving. She saw that the dust lay thick on the high, high shelf.

"You honor my shop," the shopkeeper said.

Then Miyoko heard a second voice, a voice that she had heard often before.

"Mr. Yamamoto," Grandmother said. She seemed to be looking everywhere. She seemed to miss nothing—the bright paper parasols, the folding screens, the butterfly kites, the bird cages, the teakettles on a bamboo pole.

Then she looked straight at Miyoko. She looked a long time before she spoke.

"I observe the bride doll," she said to Mr. Yamamoto, the shopkeeper. "She looks very much like one I have at home."

Mr. Yamamoto scratched his head and scowled.

"Where did I get that bride doll?" he muttered to himself.

Miyoko felt like giggling, but her face was as still as a
painted mask.

The shopkeeper bowed. "Would you like to see the
dolls, perhaps?"

"Oh, not me, please," Miyoko thought. "Not me!"

"I would not care to buy another bride doll,"
Grandmother said. "But the bridegroom doll with the
little fan in his hand—perhaps he would be a companion
to the doll I have at home."

"Allow me to remove the doll from the shelf," Mr.
Yamamoto said.

Grandmother held the bridegroom doll in her hands.
"A fine doll," she said.

Miyoko watched from the top shelf. She saw Grandmother hesitate before she handed Husband to the shopkeeper.

"In our house we have many dolls," Grandmother said. "I will not buy another doll for this festival. Another year, perhaps." She looked at the teakettles on the bamboo pole. "I wish to buy a teakettle," she said.

Miyoko watched while the shopkeeper wrapped the teakettle and tied the package with red and white cords.

The wind chimes tinkled and the shopkeeper set the bridegroom doll back on the shelf.

Miyoko watched, without blinking an eyelash, as Mr. Yamamoto sat down on the floor beside a stack of white bowls.

He closed his eyes and she knew that he slept.

Husband spoke very softly. "I have never forgotten you, Miyoko," he said, "never for one moment of these long years that we were parted."

"It is good to hear you speak so," Miyoko whispered. "The time has been so very, very long. Now that the shopkeeper sleeps, will you come with me? Will you come with me to the house of the grandmother — she whom you saw here?"

"But Miyoko," Husband said, "you do not understand. I cannot leave. I am bound to the shopkeeper who bought me. I cannot leave until I am honorably sold, until someone pays the price on the tag that is clipped to my kimono."

Miyoko clasped and unclasped her hands.

"Then I cannot leave without you," she said.

Grandmother looked down the pleasant avenue lined
with trees. "I believe I shall walk and enjoy the day,"
she said.

Her wooden sandals creaked. Kring-krong.
Kring-krong. She thought of Suzu waiting patiently at
home. She remembered that she had said she might
take a surprise home to her.

She wondered whether or not to turn back. Perhaps
Suzu would like a tiny parasol for the bride doll.

Grandmother thought of the Festival of the Dolls. She thought back to a long time ago when she, too, was a small girl who waited eagerly for the festival. Then she turned around and went back along the way she had come, to the shop where Mr. Yamamoto sat napping.

The wind chimes tinkled and Mr. Yamamoto awakened.

Miyoko peeked over the edge of the shelf and saw
Grandmother.

"I return to buy a gift for my granddaughter,"
Grandmother said. She looked around the shop.

"Would she like a small fish?" the shopkeeper asked.
"Or a turtle, perhaps?" He hesitated. "The bridegroom
doll?"

Miyoko felt faint. "Please, please, Oba-chan," she
thought, "buy Husband. Please, please."

"It grows late," said Grandmother. She looked up at the shelf. "May I look again at the doll with the fan in his hands?"

She looked at the bridegroom doll. "He is covered with dust and cobwebs," she said, "but he is much like a doll that I remember . . ."

While Grandmother stood there trying to decide what to do, Miyoko was very, very still, as only a doll can be.

At home, Suzu sat in the garden by the small pool, waiting for the sound of the jinrickisha that would bring Grandmother home.

She watched the sky for a sign of the bronze crane, and the air felt cool on her face, and her hair blew against her cheeks.

Suddenly, Suzu heard a whirr in the air. The crane flew
past and swooped into the house. Suzu rushed after
him. He was lighting on the table. And there was Miyoko,
with wisps of black hair over her eyes.

"I have returned home," she said.

"Oh, I'm so glad that you're here before Grandmother,"
Suzu said. "I've been waiting and watching for you!
Oh, your face! Your hair!" She wiped a smudge from
the small nose and tucked back the wisps of black hair.

"We flew oh-so-quickly," Miyoko said, "for the
grandmother comes in the jinrickisha, not far behind."

Miyoko stepped on the platform where she had always stood as long as Suzu could remember.

"Did you find the bridegroom doll?" Suzu asked.

"The panel, please," the bride doll said. "Slide the panel into place, Suzu. There is not much time left. Quickly, quickly, please."

As Suzu slid the front panel down, she asked, "Did you forget about the bridegroom, Miyoko? Did you forget?"

Just then, Grandmother's sandals creaked beside the
pool, and Suzu ran to greet her.

"I have returned home," Grandmother said.

Suzu helped her change into soft slippers.

Grandmother had two packages. "One package holds a
teakettle that we need," she said. "The second package
is a small surprise for you."

They walked into the house. "You may open your
package now," Grandmother said.

Suzu bowed twice. "Thank you, Oba-chan."

She unfastened the cords, and slowly laid back the folds of paper to make the surprise last longer. At last, there it was . . .

A smiling bridegroom doll, whose eyes were dark as the sky at night, looked at her. As she held him in her arms, he seemed to look past her, straight at the case that held the bride doll.

"I found him high on a shelf at Mr. Yamamoto's," Grandmother said.

Suzu could not speak because of the excitement within her. The bridegroom doll, from Mr. Yamamoto's. She leaned close against Grandmother.

"I am glad that you like the surprise," said Grandmother.

"Thank you, thank you!" Suzu said. "You are the dearest grandmother in the world." Suzu could not remember ever being so happy. She was happy for herself, but most of all, she was happy for Miyoko, the bride doll.

Suzu dusted the bridegroom and washed the dirt from his face and hands. She combed his hair with a small comb.

"See how beautiful he looks," she said, "with the dust brushed away. Look at the silk of his kimono, shining as the wing of a blackbird. Look at his lovely face." Suzu was sure the bridegroom smiled.

Grandmother laughed. "And I have yet another surprise for you," she said. "This day I learned that our bride doll is not the only one of her kind. At Mr. Yamamoto's I saw another doll exactly like her. She is not so rare as I supposed. I am giving you the bride doll, which I have had since I was just your age. That is the second surprise."

Suzu caught her breath. "But Oba-chan." She looked into Grandmother's smiling face and wondered how to make her understand. "It *is* as you thought. Our bride doll *is* the only bride doll. You see, she spoke to me. She told me she wanted to go to town. Then the bronze crane came to life. . ."

Grandmother looked at her with eyes that twinkled.

Suzu tried again. "Really, Oba-chan, the bride doll spoke to me . . ."

Grandmother laughed and stopped Suzu's speech with fingers against her lips. "You have been dreaming," she said. "When you dream a story, it becomes a tale to share, and that is proper. You may remove the doll from the case when you wish." Then Grandmother turned away and went out into the garden.

Suzu knelt beside the table and lifted the front panel of the case.

"When you dream a story," Grandmother had said. Suzu wondered if she had truly dreamed. She looked at the crane, but he was as still as only a bronze crane can be.

She looked at the bridegroom doll with his sparkling eyes and his cherry-red smile.

She looked at the bride doll with her face white as chalk and her hair like wet black paint.

"Perhaps I dreamed," Suzu whispered.

Then she looked at the hem of the bride's silk kimono, and saw that it was dingy with the dust of the high shelf in the shop where the wind chimes tinkled. Suzu pressed the palms of her hands together and her heart was joyous.

She reached for the bride doll. Tenderly, she brushed
the dust from the hem of her kimono. Lovingly, she
set Miyoko and her bridegroom on the shelf between the
cherry and the orange trees.

Then she sat on a floor cushion and whispered,
"Tomorrow we will all celebrate the festival together."

The next day Suzu served the tiny green rice cakes to each doll.

First she served the royal dolls on the highest shelf. Then she served the little ladies-in-waiting on the shelf below. Five little rice cakes she gave to the five musician dolls.

Then she served Maya, the littlest doll, and Tsuyako, the laughing-eyed doll, and Sachiko with the beautiful hair. There were three crumbs for the bronze crane. Last of all, she served Miyoko and Husband, leaning close to them.

"Welcome, Bridegroom, to the Festival of the Dolls," she said. "Welcome, Miyoko, to the Festival of the Dolls. My heart is happy."

There was no answer. "Do you hear me, Miyoko?" she asked.

For a moment, it seemed to Suzu that the bride doll smiled and nodded her head ever so slightly. But when she looked again, Miyoko was still—very, very still— as only a doll can be.

This edition lithographed in U. S. A. by Wetzel Bros., Inc., Milwaukee 2, Wisconsin